T0037328
Polly
Pomegr
Belinda
Blackcurrant
Alice Apple
Peter
Potato
Grace Grape
Wee Willie
Water Melon

The Garden Gang
Stories and pictures by
Jayne Fisher

Other Garden Gang stories

Series 793

Penelope Strawberry and Roger Radish

Percival Pea and Polly Pomegranate

Oliver Onion and Tim Tomato

Wee Willie Water Melon and Betty Beetroot

Lucy Leek and Bertie Brussels Sprout

Gertrude Gooseberry and Belinda Blackcurrant

Peter Potato and Alice Apple

Pam Parsnip and Lawrence Lemon

Grace Grape and Robert Raspberry

Sheila Shallot and Benny Broad Bean

Avril Apricot and Simon Swede

Colin Cucumber

Ladybird Books Loughborough

Colin Cucumber
couldn't cry,
even though
his leg hurt very much.
He had accidentally
fallen over a brick
which someone had
carelessly left lying
on the garden path.
"I hope someone
comes along soon
to help me up,"
he thought.

Roger Radish
came skipping happily
along the garden path
whistling to himself,
as he often did.
Suddenly he saw
poor Colin sitting
on the ground
looking very sorry
for himself.
"I've hurt my leg,"
he moaned,
"and I can't stand up."
Roger dashed off
to get help.

Mark Marrow
was crossing the lawn.
"Help!" called Roger.
"Colin Cucumber
has hurt his leg.
Come quickly!"
Mark hurried
to where Colin
was sitting on the path.
He knew exactly
what to do.
"Go and ring
for an ambulance
and I will get
a warm blanket," he said.

Roger went to a
nearby telephone box
and dialled the number.
"I want an ambulance,
quickly," he said.
"Please send it to the
corner of the garden
where the
Garden Gang live."
He put down
the telephone and
ran back to the path
where he found Colin
snugly wrapped
in a warm blanket.

Quite a crowd
had gathered
by this time.
They all looked worried
and chatted quietly
to each other.
Colin's leg was not
hurting quite so much
and he looked
much more cheerful.
Between you and me,
I think by now
he was quite enjoying
all the fuss!

Soon an ambulance
came racing along
the garden path
with its sirens blaring.
As it stopped
beside the small crowd,
two tomatoes
jumped out
with a stretcher
and gently lifted Colin
into the back of
the ambulance.
Mark Marrow
also climbed in
to keep him company.
The doors were closed
and away they went.

AMBULANCE

It wasn't long
before they reached
the hospital,
and Colin Cucumber
found himself riding
on a trolley into the
X-ray department.
''We are just going to
take a picture of your leg
to see if any
bones are broken,''
said a kind nurse.
''It will only
take a minute.''

How Colin and Mark
laughed
when they
saw the picture.
They could see
right through Colin's leg.
They could also see
a small crack
in the bone.
''It's not too serious,''
said the doctor.
''But we will put
a pot on your leg
to make sure
it heals quickly.''

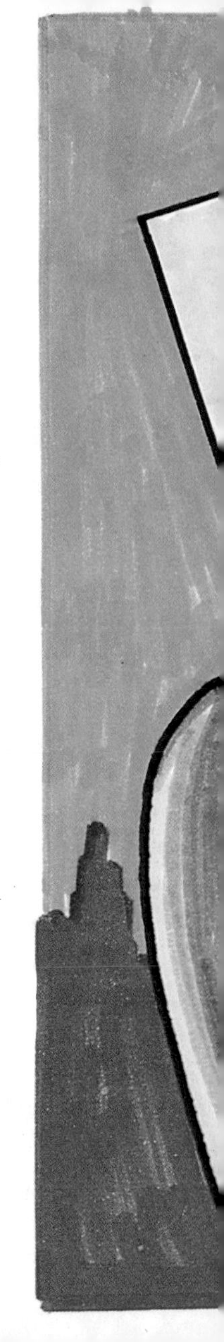

Colin looked quite funny
lying in bed
with his pot leg in the air.
Mark was allowed
to stay and talk to him.
''You can
go home tomorrow,''
said the doctor.
''We just want to
make sure that your pot
sets correctly.''

The next morning
an ambulance
took Colin Cucumber
back to the garden
where all his friends
were waiting to greet him.
''It's nice to be back,''
he said, shyly,
as he grinned round
at everyone.
''I have to go back
to the hospital
in six weeks
to have the pot
taken off.''

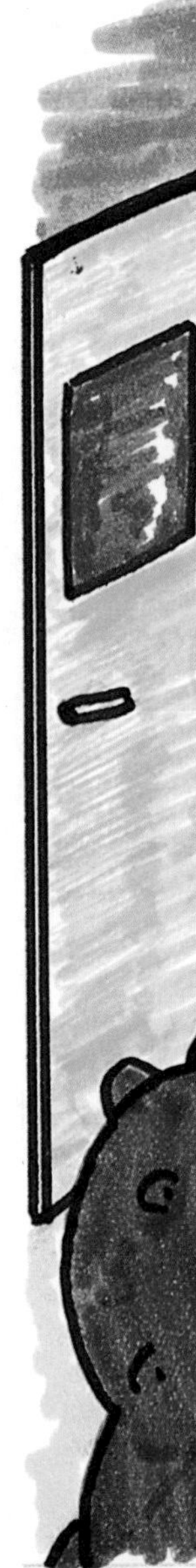

ACCIDENT

When the six weeks
were up, Colin went
back to the hospital.
He worried a little
when the pot
first came off
and the doctor
asked him to stand up.
But soon he realised,
to his delight, that...

F
PJ
BANDAGES
Medicine
2
REPORT

his leg was . . .

as good as new !

Patrick Pear

Patrick Pear
loved to fish.
He had a
beautiful fishing rod
and a good strong net,
of which he was
very proud.
His fishing began
in the morning
and carried on
through to the evening.
Sometimes he would fish
through the night.
But he never
caught anything.

One morning
there had been
a rain storm
and Patrick Pear
hurriedly pulled on
his fine, blue
wellington boots
and grabbed
his fishing tackle.
He dashed outside
and began to fish
in the many puddles
left by the rain.
Although he fished all day,
he didn't catch anything.

Another time,
Mr Rake, the gardener,
left a watering can
full of water
on the garden path.
Patrick Pear
immediately got out
his fishing rod
and began to fish
in the can of water.
Two hours went by
before Mr Rake
returned for his can,
but poor Patrick
didn't catch anything.

The ornamental fountain
often attracted Patrick.
He would sit for hours
on the rim,
smiling to himself,
whilst he dangled his line
hopefully into
the clear, cool waters.
He became soaked,
and his wellingtons
squelched with water.
But the only thing
he ever caught there
was a cold.

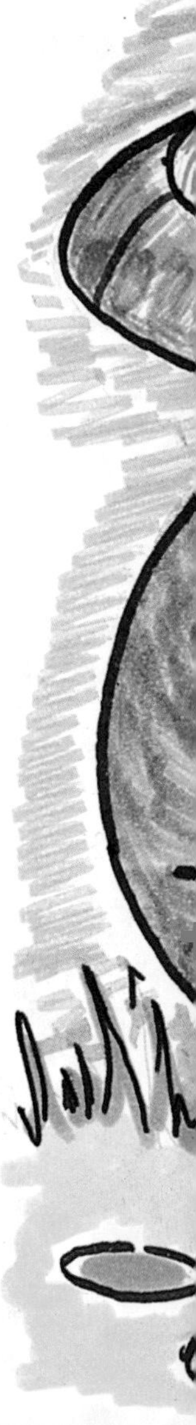

As the sun shone brightly
one afternoon,
the gardener's daughter
left her cup of hot tea
on the wall top
whilst she went to look
at a gorgeous butterfly.
Before you could say,
'Flying fish',
Patrick was about to
lower his line
into the cup
when, luckily,
the girl returned
and he ran off.

It was early Autumn.
Already, the leaves
were beginning to
change colour
and the swallows
were gathering together
making ready to fly
to warmer countries.
Miss Delia Damson
decided to call
a meeting of the
Garden Gang Committee.
''Be at the greenhouse
by six o'clock,'' she said.
''I have an idea
I want to discuss.''

By six o'clock
that evening
the Garden Gang
were standing excitedly
outside the greenhouse.
''This is my idea,''
said Miss Delia Damson.
''I think that
the Garden Gang should
be taken on a day trip
to the seaside
before winter.
Is it a good idea?''
she asked.
''Yes, yes!'' they all cried
and began to make
immediate plans.

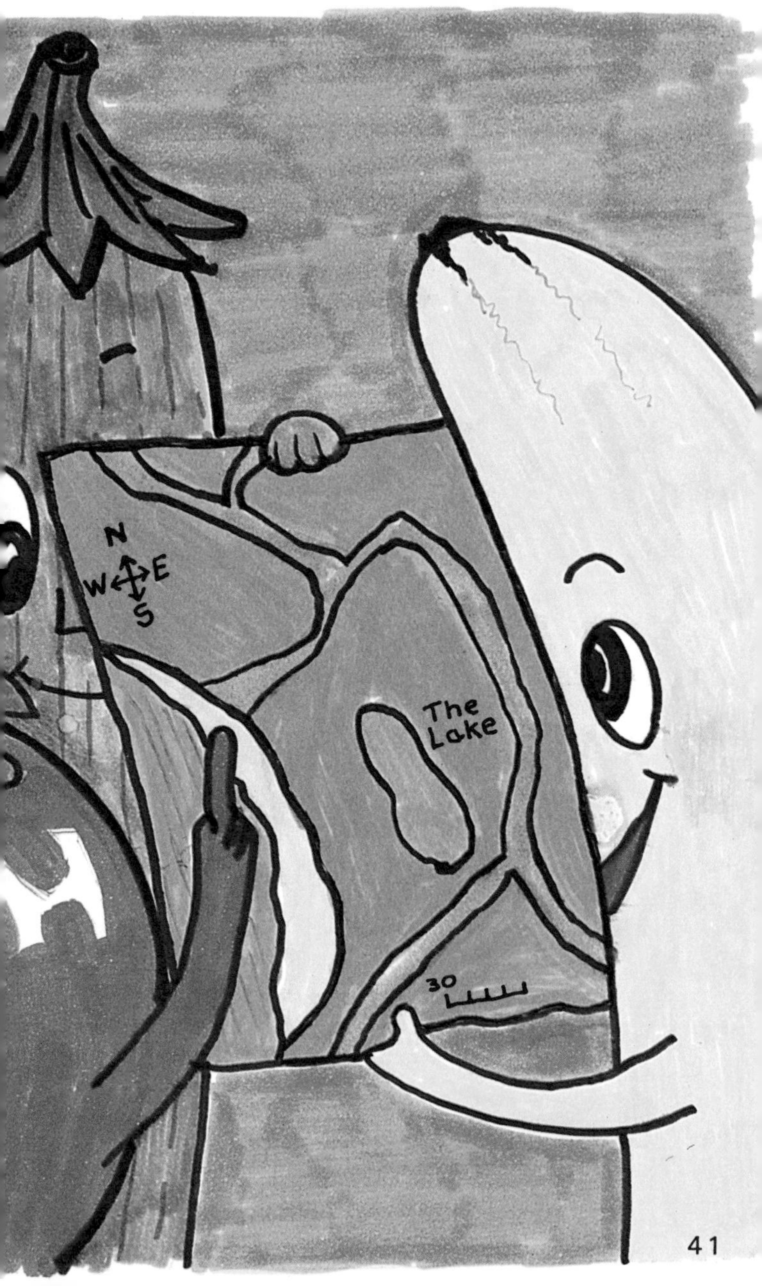
N
W
E
S
The Lake
30

It was decided
that they should hire
Cardew Carrot's blue bus
and that they should take
a picnic tea.
"I will buy everyone
an icecream,"
said Penelope Strawberry
and they all
smiled at her, shyly.
"Please may I take
my fishing rod?" said
Patrick's small voice
from the back.
"Of course," they said.

It was a beautiful day
as the Garden Gang
packed themselves
into Cardew's bus.
The chattering and
laughing could be heard
all over the garden.
When they finally set off,
Patrick's fishing rod
was sticking out of
the sunshine roof.
There was
no room inside for it.

Soon they were
at the seaside.
The bus door opened
and they all spilled out
onto the seashore.
There were
donkeys to ride,
boats to row,
and candy floss
and icecream to eat.
But you can all guess
what Patrick did
can't you?
That's right,
he went to the sea
and began to fish.

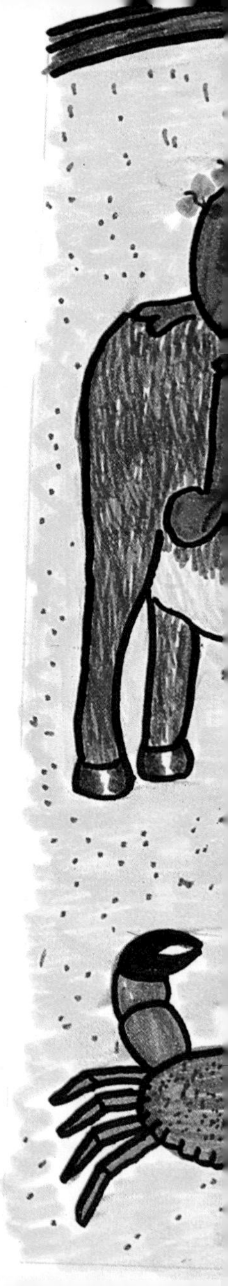

A crowd of sleepy
but very happy
fruit and vegetable people
slowly climbed
into the blue bus.
It was evening
and everyone
was ready for home.
What a wonderful day
it had been.
"Where's Patrick?"
they all called.
"Here he comes,"
said Cardew.
Patrick was wearing
an enormous smile
and carrying...

9

a fish!

Bertie Brussels Sprout
Paul Pumpkin
Mark Marrow
Tim Tomato
Patrick Pear